The Animal Adventure Club series

The Baby Deer Rescue (book 1)
The Baby Otter Rescue (book 2)
The Baby Red Squirrel Rescue (book 3)

For Nell – M.S.
For Clementine, with all my love – H.G.

Kelpies is an imprint of Floris Books. First published in 2020 by Floris Books
Series concept and endmatter illustrations © 2020 Floris Books.
Text © 2020 Michelle Sloan. Illustrations © 2020 Hannah George
Michelle Sloan and Hannah George have asserted their rights under the
Copyright, Designs and Patent Act 1988 to be identified as the Author and
Illustrator of this Work

 Also available as an eBook

British Library CIP data available
ISBN 978-178250-666-9
Printed in Great Britain by CPI Group (UK) Ltd, Croydon

 Floris Books supports sustainable forest management by printing this book on materials
made from wood that comes from responsible sources and reclaimed material

MIX
Paper from
responsible sources
FSC® C020471

The Baby Red Squirrel Rescue

Written by
Michelle Sloan

Illustrated by
Hannah George

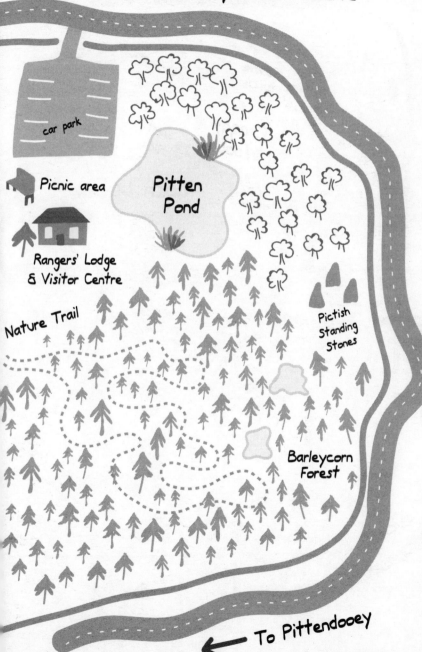

1

Isla MacLeod chewed the end of her pencil and stared out over Pittendooey Nature Reserve. The sun shimmered on Loch Dooey, swallows swooped overhead and a skylark sang in the distance. It was calm and beautiful, but a worry was bothering Isla, like a bird fluttering in her tummy.

"Hello? Earth to Isla!" said Buzz. "Do you read me?"

Isla looked at Buzz, Lexi and Gracie, the other members of the Animal Adventure Club. Her friends were all staring at her. She had been lost in thought and forgotten she was in the middle of a club meeting at a picnic table outside the rangers' lodge.

"Sorry, what?" Isla said.

"You were miles away!" said Gracie. "What were you thinking about?"

"Oh, nothing," said Isla, shaking her head. "Just daydreaming. Now, where were we?"

"You were going to read out the list of animals to go on our new poster for the information board," said Buzz. "Add midges, by the way." He swatted his hands around his face.

Isla glanced down at her list. "So, the poster about animals and birds you might spot at Pittendooey Nature Reserve will say:

- Foxes
- Hedgehogs
- Red squirrels
- Badgers
- Roe deer
- Bats
- Otters
- Owls
- Swallows
- Oystercatchers

"Is that all? I mean, they're the animals *we've* seen," said Lexi, "but there must be tonnes more!"

Gracie bit her lip. "You're right, Lexi. And we haven't even explored every single part of the nature reserve."

"We have so!" said Buzz defiantly.

"We go out on patrol at least three times a week, Gracie. We know it pretty well," said Lexi.

"Well, there's one place we've never been," said Gracie with a knowing smile.

Everyone frowned and stared at her.

"Where?" asked Isla.

"Mungo's Island!" Gracie said with a grin.

"Whose island?" said a very confused Lexi.

"Mungo's Island," said Gracie, pointing towards the loch.

They all looked out towards the small island in the middle of Loch Dooey. They could see trees and bushes tangled around a mysterious small building.

"Yeah!" said Isla. "You're right, we've never been over there."

"What is that castle thing?" Lexi asked, standing up and reaching for her binoculars.

"Oh, that's the Folly," said Buzz casually.

"The whatty?" asked Lexi, the lenses pressed to her eyes.

"Well," said Buzz, popping a custard cream in his mouth, "it's um... it's a..."

"It's a kind of giant garden decoration," Isla explained. "It was built years ago, when the nature reserve belonged to Mungo, the Laird of Dooey."

"We need to explore!" said Gracie.

"Think of all the animals living over there that we've never seen!"

"It's Saturday tomorrow. Why don't we go then?" suggested Buzz.

"Great idea," agreed Lexi enthusiastically.

"And camp!" added Gracie. "We could track animals, use camouflage and maybe even build a den?"

"Yay!" they all shouted, Lexi loudest of all. Everyone put their fingers in their ears.

"Is this an Animal Adventure Club meeting or a party?" asked Lisa, Pittendooey's ranger and Lexi's auntie. She was walking towards the lodge, carrying a large crate. "I could hear you from down the road! What's all the excitement?"

"Can we camp out on Mungo's Island on Saturday night, Lisa?" asked Lexi. "Go on, say yes, pretty please!" She gave Lisa a big hug.

"If all your parents agree, that would be an excellent plan," said Lisa, putting down the crate. "I was over on the island a couple of days ago and it's a lovely safe place to pitch a tent. I can camp on this side of the loch so you can have an adult nearby."

Suddenly, there was a scuffling noise coming from inside the crate.

"What's in there, Lisa?" asked Isla, walking over to inspect it.

"I have a surprise! And it'll tie in nicely with your camping plan too." Through the bars, the Animal Adventure Club could see three small, dark chestnut-brown, fluffy creatures with round chubby faces, long teeth and twitching whiskers. Everyone gasped.

"What are those?" asked Lexi. "Rats?"

"No, they're water voles, and we're going to release them into the loch this weekend! There are two more arriving tomorrow."

"Oh wow!" beamed Isla. "That's so exciting! I've never seen a water vole."

"I've been looking for a habitat for them, and the steep grassy bank and reeds on the west side of Mungo's Island is ideal," Lisa explained.

"Can we help?" asked Gracie.

"I think this would be a perfect project for the Animal Adventure Club," said Lisa, cheekily snatching the last biscuit from the picnic table. "Water voles are a protected species, so you can monitor their progress and report back."

"We'll be the Water Vole Patrol!" said Buzz.

"Awesome! Let's start planning!" said Gracie.

"You guys should start by making a list of camping supplies," said Lisa. "And remember, there probably won't be a mobile phone signal on Mungo's Island.

I've got walkie-talkies you could take. I know they work out there, so we can keep in touch."

"Och, it's not a problem, Lisa. I know Morse code," said Gracie. "I can flash my torch on and off to spell out words and send messages."

"Morse code?" giggled Buzz. "That's soooo old-fashioned!"

Gracie frowned and folded her arms.

"Buzz, don't be rude. It's a good idea, Gracie, but let's hope we don't have to use it." Lisa put her arm around Gracie's shoulder.

Isla started to write their list, forgetting her worries for now.

TO DO LIST

- Research water voles.

- Go shopping for food: baked beans, sausages, rolls, fruit, custard creams.

- Pack camping stuff: tents, sleeping bags, pillows.

2

Later that Friday, Isla peered into the cage where her pet mice, Tattie and Bogle, lived. There were so many twisty tunnels that it looked like a mouse adventure playground. But Tattie wasn't running around. He was just sitting on a pile of shredded paper, looking sorry for himself.

"He doesn't seem right, does he, Mum?" said Isla.

Mum gave Isla a hug. "Maybe Tattie's got a wee cold," she said. "Remember Bogle was a bit under the weather a few weeks ago? He soon got better."

Isla opened the cage, reached in and gently lifted out Tattie. She looked him over carefully. He was a lovely sandy colour with a pink nose. His long, twitching whiskers drooped slightly at the ends, and his eyes were watery. He suddenly let out a tiny sneeze.

"Why don't you call Buzz?" asked Mum. "You know he loves mice. He might be able to help."

"No," said Isla. "He'll tell me to take Tattie to the vet, and I don't want to do that. Just in case..."

"Just in case what?" said Mum, stroking Isla's hair.

"In case we find out that Tattie's really sick." Isla's eyes filled with tears. She whispered gently to Tattie, then popped him back in the cage. He snuggled into his bedding and closed his eyes.

Mum watched as Isla washed her hands and then sat down miserably at the kitchen table.

"I know you're worried," said Mum, "but you can't bury your head in the sand. How about I take him to the vet this afternoon while you get ready for camping tomorrow. It'll take your mind off things."

Isla nodded. A big tear rolled down her cheek.

Suddenly the doorbell rang and a funny voice shouted through the letterbox. "Hell-oo?! Isla MacLeod!"

Isla and her mum looked at each other and smiled. "Come in, Gracie Munroe!" Isla shouted back, wiping away a tear. The front door opened and Gracie came bounding into the kitchen. She was wearing shorts, welly boots and a T-shirt with a grizzly bear on it, and had a huge grin on her face.

"Right, are you ready to pack? I can't wait for our island adventure! It's totally my thing, I'm going to..." She stopped and looked curiously at Isla's puffy eyes. "Are you OK, Isla?"

"Yes, she is," said Isla's mum, ruffling

Isla's hair. "Now, Isla, you need to get organised. Your sleeping bag is in your bedroom cupboard. The tent is under the stairs, but check all the pegs are there! You don't want to get out to Mungo's Island then discover half of them are missing."

"I'd just make us a den for the night," said Gracie with a shrug of her shoulders, and Mum laughed.

"Right, let's get started," said Isla, standing up and giving herself a shake.

"I've made a list to tick off as we go," said Gracie, pulling out a notepad from her pocket. "Buzz helped," she added.

- Tents (and pegs!) x 2
- Mallet for banging in pegs
- Sleeping bags x 4
- Sleeping mats x 4
- Pillows x 4

- Torch (I'll bring my head torch)

- First aid kit

- Walkie-talkie

- Binoculars

- Insect repellent

- Flasks x 4

- Food! Rolls, butter, sausages, baked beans, fruit. **Custard creams!**

"Great!" said Isla. "Let's go shopping first, then we can get packing. We'll see you in a bit, Mum."

Isla threw one more mournful look at Tattie's cage before she and Gracie headed out and down Pittendooey Main Street towards the little supermarket.

"I can tell something's up," said Gracie, slipping her arm through Isla's.

"I'm fine," said Isla, pretending everything was OK.

Gracie stopped and turned to look at her friend. "Isla, you can tell me if something's upsetting you. It's not good to bottle up your worries."

Isla nodded sheepishly. "It's Tattie," she admitted. "I'm scared that something's wrong with him."

"Have you taken him to the vet?" asked Gracie.

"Mum's going to take him this afternoon," Isla said.

"That's the best thing to do. Try not to worry," said Gracie, taking Isla's hand in hers.

"Thanks, Gracie, I feel better just having told you."

"That's what friends are for!" Gracie gave Isla's hand a squeeze.

3

The next day was Saturday: time for the camping trip! It was a bright, sunny afternoon at Pittendooey Nature Reserve, and the loch was calm and still.

"This crate is pretty heavy considering there are only three wee water voles inside!" said Buzz. He and Lexi held one side each, carrying it carefully down to the boat sheds. Isla and Gracie carried another crate. Every so often there was a squeak and a bump as the water voles moved around.

"I know!" said Gracie. "We've only got two and my arms are aching!"

"Any news on Tattie, Isla?" asked Buzz, swatting his hand around. "Ugh, these midges!"

"The vet said he's got an infection and has given him some medicine," Isla sighed.

"Poor Tattie!" said Lexi. "He's adorable."

Isla was pale, and her eyes were a bit red, as though she'd been crying.

"Try not to worry," Gracie said.

Isla gave her a little smile. "These wee water voles and our camping trip will keep my mind off things," she said.

"We should be taking fishing rods," said Buzz. "There's plenty of trout in Loch Dooey."

"Ew!" said Lexi. "No way! I'll stick with my flask of baked beans, thank you very much!"

Lisa was waiting for them at the boat sheds with all their camping gear. After they'd put the crates down carefully, she helped them into life jackets.

"Right, let's go through some safety reminders," Lisa said. "Life jackets must be worn at all times. No standing up when the boat is moving, store the oars properly when you're not using them, and dock the boat with the correct knot when you land on Mungo's Island, the way I showed you earlier. Lexi, are you paying attention?"

Lexi was kneeling down beside the crates and peering through the mesh on one side. "I know I say this about almost every animal I see," she said, "but these water rats, I mean voles, are the *cutest things I've ever seen!*"

Lisa rolled her eyes. "They are cute, Lexi," she said, "but remember..."

"I know, I know," sighed Lexi, standing up again. "They're wild animals."

"Here's the walkie-talkie I promised you," said Lisa. Gracie reached out to take it and placed it carefully beside their food supplies.

"Right, let's get going!" said Lisa. "Help me load the crates into my boat first, please. I can take your camping gear too."

Lisa clambered into the boat, and Buzz and Lexi handed her the two water-vole crates. Then in a human chain, they all passed the camping gear. Once the boat was loaded, Gracie untied it and shoved it away from the pier. Lisa reached for the oars and began slicing them through the still water.

"See you at the other side!" she called.

"Right, our turn," said Buzz, awkwardly climbing into the boat, which tipped under his weight.

"Woah!" giggled Lexi. "Falling in wouldn't be the best start, Buzz!"

Buzz chuckled. "Pass me the food bag and the walkie-talkie. I'll keep them safe at my feet."

"Oof, that bag is so heavy!" Lexi hauled the bag over to Buzz. "Is that a biscuit tin in there? We're only going for a night!"

"We've got to be prepared, Lexi," said

Buzz, grinning. "I'm feeling pretty hungry already!"

They all clambered in and settled themselves onto the benches, then Lexi untethered the boat. Pushing away, Buzz and Gracie rowed off. At first they just went round in a circle. Everyone giggled as they practised getting the boat to go in the right direction, but soon Buzz and Gracie found their rhythm and everyone was beaming.

"Looking good, guys!" shouted Lisa from her boat.

"I wonder what animals we might find on the island?" said Isla.

"I don't know, Isla, but I can't wait to find out!" said Gracie gazing out at Mungo's Island. "It's going to be the best night ever!"

4

Soon the Animal Adventure Club's boat reached Mungo's Island and Lisa helped them all out.

"It's exciting and scary at the same time," said Lexi helping to unload. "I mean, we're going to be here all night, on our own!"

"We'll be fine," said Gracie. "Remember, you've got a survival expert with you: me!"

"First, get your boat tied up," said Lisa. "That old tree there looks good, Gracie. Then we'll release the water voles into their new home."

Gracie wrapped the rope around the

tree. "I'm going to tie a different knot than the one you showed us, Lisa. I think it'll hold better," she said.

"Er, shouldn't we do exactly what Lisa told us?" asked Buzz.

Gracie made a face at him.

"Buzz, Gracie knows every knot there is!" said Isla.

"It's OK with me," said Lisa. "I trust you, Gracie, survival expert!"

They set off with Lisa and Isla carrying one crate and Lexi and Buzz the other.

"We know water voles used to live here because we can see their old burrows," explained Lisa, leading them round to the far side of Mungo's Island. "The burrows should help them settle in. There's lots of tasty vegetation growing in the loch, so they'll like that too."

"How will we keep an eye on them?" asked Isla.

"We'll do regular field observations," Lisa began. "We can monitor their eating habits by looking at nibbled vegetation. Water voles bite the stems at a 45-degree angle and leave them in a neat pile. We can look for their droppings too."

"They look like Tic Tacs!" said Gracie, running up to join them.

"Ew!" said Lexi. "Why do you always compare animal poo to food, Gracie?"

"They have a wee toilet area outside their burrows," added Gracie, ignoring

Lexi. "Their little piles of poo are called 'latrines'!"

"Hey," said Buzz suddenly, "what's that in the water?" He pointed and they all stared out over the loch.

Something was swimming away from the island towards the mainland. Every so often they could see a flash of reddish fur.

"It can't be..." said Lisa. "Can I borrow someone's binoculars?"

Buzz quickly passed his to Lisa and she put the lenses to her eyes.

"Isla, now you look and tell me what you see," said Lisa, with a huge grin.

Isla peered through the binoculars, then took them away and stared at Lisa.

"A red squirrel!" Isla said in disbelief. "Swimming!"

"No way!" said Gracie, taking the binoculars next.

Sure enough, there was a red squirrel swimming across Loch Dooey!

"How funny!" said Lexi. "What's it doing that for?"

Lisa explained, "Actually, squirrels are strong swimmers. It's just that we hardly ever see them doing it."

"Maybe it's just keeping fit!" laughed Buzz.

They took turns with the binoculars until the squirrel made it to the other side of the loch. Then it scurried up a tree and vanished into Craggy Woods.

"Wow!" Isla gasped. "It's rare to spot a red squirrel, never mind one swimming!"

"Yup, and I'm really glad the Animal Adventure Club got to see it! That's a once-in-a-lifetime chance, I reckon," said Lisa. "I wonder if it came over when the water level was low a few weeks back and the causeway appeared. It could have run over to the island."

"Huh?" said Lexi. "What's the causeway?"

"It's a sort of bridge that people used to walk over to the island," Lisa explained. She drew a picture in the sand.

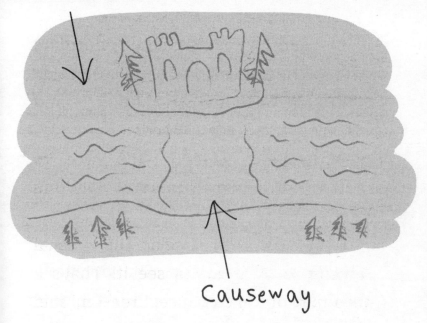

Low water

Causeway

"Then the water level in the loch got higher and the causeway disappeared underwater," Gracie chipped in, drawing little waves of water.

"But it sometimes reappears when we've not had much rain," Buzz added, smoothing Gracie's waves and redrawing the causeway. "Like a few weeks ago."

"Just long enough for a squirrel to dash over and enjoy all the pine cones and snacks on the island!" said Lisa.

They were interrupted by squeaks from the crates.

"The water voles are getting impatient," laughed Buzz.

"Right," said Lisa, "let's get them out!"

"Here goes," said Isla. She unclipped the doors of the crates and lifted some of the straw. Soon the little fluffy creatures scuttled out and sniffed the air, their whiskers twitching.

"Wow, they're so cute!" said Lexi, pulling out her sketchbook. She loved drawing and always had pencils and paper close to hand. She drew as the water voles ambled around, taking their time to get used to their new home.

"They look like mini beavers, especially their teeth," observed Isla, who then looked over Lexi's shoulder at her drawing. "It's brilliant, Lexi!"

"Thanks!" Lexi beamed.

"Wow, they look like Ratty from *The Wind in the Willows!*" said Buzz. "He was actually a water vole."

Without warning, one water vole jumped in the loch with a plop. It began to swim through the reeds that poked up out of the water in a fast-paced zigzag. Then, one after another, they all followed and were gone.

"That went well," said Gracie. "Welcome to Pittendooey Nature Reserve, wee friends!"

"We can monitor them here and check for them on the other side of the loch," said Lisa. "We could even set up a special raft to check their droppings."

"Ew!" grumbled Lexi.

"It sounds like fun. We can look for their footprints too!" said Isla.

"Their paw prints are like wee star shapes," said Gracie. "The size of a 5p!"

"We'll leave the crates here in case the voles want somewhere safe to pop back to," said Lisa. "Now, I guess I should leave you to set up for the night!"

"Yes, please," blurted Gracie excitedly. "Sorry, Lisa, no offence, but we can't wait to have the island to ourselves!"

After one last safety check, and a reminder that she would be camping just over the loch, near the boat sheds, Lisa rowed away, giving the Animal Adventure Club a cheery wave. They grinned at each other. Alone at last!

5

As Lisa rowed back to the boat sheds on the other side of the loch, the Animal Adventure Club wondered what to do first now that they were by themselves on Mungo's Island.

"Who's ready for a snack?" asked Buzz. He delved into the food bag and pulled out the tin of biscuits. They all grabbed a couple and sat munching as they looked at their surroundings.

"Let's explore!" said Lexi. "Then we can set up the tents."

"We should pitch our tents now," said Gracie. "It's best to do that straight away, particularly while it's nice and dry. You know that the weather in Scotland can change quickly."

"Och, no!" said Buzz. "The weather's fine, Gracie. Let's explore! We've got plenty of time."

Isla noticed Gracie biting her lip, and she could tell her friend was worried.

"It won't take long to look around," she said reassuringly.

"OK then," Gracie agreed, giving a small smile.

They all headed over to the tower-shaped Folly, which stood on a mound at the north end of Mungo's Island. Several tall trees had grown around it.

"It's like a mini castle," said Isla.

"Maybe there's been a princess sleeping inside for one hundred years!" laughed

Buzz, pretending to slash at branches with an imaginary sword.

Suddenly, something dashed past them through the undergrowth.

"What was that?" gasped Lexi.

"I didn't see anything," said Gracie.

Lexi's eyes were as wide as saucers, and she shivered. "I hope we haven't disturbed a spooky spirit by coming to the island!"

Gracie pulled a face and shook her head. "I don't think so, Lexi."

"It was a tiny animal – probably a mouse or a shrew," said Buzz. "I saw it out of the corner of my eye."

The Folly had an archway for a door and there was no glass in the windows. The needles and branches of a large Scots pine tree swept and twisted over the stones.

"It looks so old and creepy," muttered Lexi.

Gracie strolled right up and stuck her head through an empty window. "It smells a bit fusty," she said, "but there's nothing inside apart from moss, grass and – oh!"

"What?" asked Lexi, her voice trembling.

"Come and see!" said Gracie.

Buzz and Isla pushed through the branches and undergrowth, but Lexi stayed back.

"What is it?" asked Buzz.

"Owl pellets!" said Gracie. "I think the Folly is home to an owl!"

"Ooh," said Isla, coming for a closer look. "What kind of owl?"

"I think it's a barn owl," Gracie replied, poking at the pellet with her stick.

"Is a pellet another kind of poo?" shouted Lexi from outside the Folly. "What does this one smell like, Gracie? Chocolate? Coffee?" Lexi followed the others inside.

Gracie rolled her eyes. "A pellet isn't a poo, Lexi. It's undigested food that the owl coughs back up. You know, like bones or bits of beak."

yuck!

"Amazing!" said Buzz.

"I'm going to take this and dissect it," said Gracie, picking it up with a tissue and popping the pellet carefully in her pocket.

"Ew!" shrieked Lexi. "Isn't that a bit gross?"

"Not really," said Gracie casually. "If we pick it apart, we can tell what this owl has been eating."

Suddenly a flash of red caught Isla's eye. She grabbed Gracie, who was still telling Lexi all about pellets, and pointed upwards.

"Look!" Isla whispered. Everyone's eyes followed her pointing hand. "There's your 'spooky spirit', Lexi!"

Peering down at them from the very top of the Folly was a tiny red squirrel. It had tufty, rusty orange ears and a creamy white tummy. Its tail was like a feather duster and its fur ruffled in the breeze. It tipped its head to one side and looked back at the Animal Adventure Club.

Lexi clamped her hand over her mouth to muffle a squeal. "It's so cute!" she whispered through her hands.

"It's a kit," Isla explained quietly. "A baby red squirrel. It looks like it's only a few weeks old."

"Wow, it's so... *red*!" said Gracie. "As red as a chilli pepper!"

"Wait, look!" said Isla. "There's another one! And another!"

Two more baby red squirrels had scampered over to stare down at them.

"Chilli, and now Spice and Scarlet!" chuckled Lexi. "We should rename this place Red Squirrel Island!"

Three identical, inquisitive fluffy faces stared down at them. Then, with a flick of their tails, they darted away.

"Look, there's their drey in the fork of the Scots pine branches," said Isla, pointing upwards.

"Is a drey their nest?" asked Lexi.

"Yes, it's about the size of a football. It's made of twigs, with leaves and moss inside to keep them cosy."

"Maybe the red squirrel we saw swimming away was their mum..." Buzz suggested.

"That wouldn't be good," said Isla. "These kits are way too young to be looking after themselves."

"Hopefully she'll come back," said Gracie.

They were quietly thinking about this when large raindrops began to fall. First there were just a few plops, but then it was as though someone had turned on a shower.

"We were so busy looking at the squirrels we didn't notice the big dark clouds!" said Buzz.

"Oh no!" groaned Gracie. "Our camping stuff!"

The Animal Adventure Club pelted back to their gear, which was already very wet.

"Well, guys," said Gracie, trying to stay upbeat. "We'll just have to pitch our tents in the rain."

Isla was grateful Gracie didn't say, "I told you so."

"Well, at least the biscuits are nice and dry in the tin!" said Buzz.

6

Under a moody grey sky and soaking rain, the Animal Adventure Club started to pitch their tents.

"First we need to choose the right site," Gracie told them. She had been camping lots of times and knew exactly what to do.

"How about down here, near the loch?" suggested Buzz, a raindrop hanging from the end of his nose.

"What about nearer the bushes?" Gracie replied. "They'll give us shelter if the wind picks up."

"I like Buzz's idea!" said Lexi. "Then we can look out over the loch."

Gracie sighed. "I think you're making a mistake, guys. If it gets windy later it could be a problem."

"Stop worrying, it'll be fine!" said Buzz.

Gracie bit her lip, then pressed on. "Right, next we need to clear the sites ready for the tents," she said. "Check the ground for anything sharp that might puncture the ground sheet, like sticks or stones."

Once they'd cleared the ground, they laid out their tents. Then they began threading poles through the slots and banging in pegs with mallets. Buzz and Gracie were sharing one tent, and Lexi and Isla were in the other one. However, Isla was doing most of the work.

"I'm just having a wee break," said Lexi, sitting on the ground with her hood up, the rain running in little rivers down her waterproof. "It's hard work, and the midges are really going for me!" There was a small cloud of midges hovering over her head.

"You just have to..." Isla slapped a midge that was nibbling her face, "...try to ignore them."

"Um... I think we're missing some tent pegs," said Buzz, rummaging through the bag.

"But I checked before we left!" cried Gracie. She began frantically searching through the tent supplies. "Oh no," she groaned. "There was another bag of pegs, and now it's not here. How could I have lost it?"

Isla could tell Gracie was very annoyed with herself. "Don't worry," she said. "We can give you some of ours."

"But then we'll both be short on pegs." Gracie frowned.

"It'll be fine," said Isla. She looked at her tent and started giggling. "Look, Gracie, it's the tent ghost of Mungo's Island!"

Lexi, who was helping again, had got stuck inside the tent while trying to feed a pole into place.

"It's not funny!" said her muffled voice.

"It's boiling in here too!"

"At least you're not getting bitten alive by midges out here," snapped Buzz.

"Don't bet on that," Lexi replied. "The wee devils are in here too!"

Buzz batted midges away from his own face. "It's OK about the pegs, Gracie. I'm using some big, smooth stones to hold the tent down, and some sticks too."

"Maybe I should build a den!" said Gracie.

"No time for that now," groaned Lexi, finally staggering out of the tent. "I'm starving! Let's eat."

The rain had stopped, so the Animal Adventure Club sat outside their tents to eat their dinner. They knew it wasn't safe for them to light a fire without Lisa there, so they had all brought flasks filled with hot baked beans and sausages, which they ate with floury buttered rolls. For pudding, they had ripe juicy peaches.

"Eating outside always makes food taste better," said Buzz in between mouthfuls. "Thank goodness the wind has blown the midges away."

"They like you a lot, Buzz," said Gracie, gazing over at the tents, which were flapping in the wind. "You know what? I think I will build a den after dinner. And if you don't mind, Buzz, I might sleep in it too."

"Go for it!" said Buzz. "You might be a bit cold in there, though."

Gracie started building in a sheltered corner, using branches and large sticks.

Buzz looked at Lexi mischievously. "I'm sure I've heard a ghost story about Mungo. He liked to fish on the loch and he had the Folly built so he had somewhere to sit and eat his sandwiches. But he doesn't like visitors on his island, and people say you can hear him munching his sandwiches in the dead of night..."

"What?" said Lexi, going white with fear.

"Munch, munch, munch!" giggled Gracie, staggering towards Buzz and Lexi with her arms outstretched. "Get off my island, Lexi!" she said in a spooky voice.

Everyone fell about laughing – even Lexi.

By the evening, Gracie had finished her den and Isla had checked on the water voles. She hadn't spotted them, though – perhaps they were still exploring, she thought. After the Animal Adventure Club told some more silly ghost stories with their torches under their chins, they all went to bed.

Isla lay in her sleeping bag with her eyes wide open. It was windy outside now, but she wasn't worried about the noise, or even that the tent might blow away. She was worried about the red squirrel kits.

What if their mother doesn't come back? she thought. *How on earth are those little things going to survive?* Her mind drifted to her little mouse Tattie too. Isla hated it when animals were unwell or in danger. It made her feel so helpless. No matter how hard she tried to think about happy things, she just couldn't get to sleep.

"Isla? Are you awake?" Lexi whispered beside her, her sleeping bag pulled right up to her nose.

"Yes," said Isla.

"I can't sleep," admitted Lexi. "I'm a bit scared." The wind had really picked up now and was blowing the tent wildly.

"I can't sleep either," said Isla.

"You're not scared though," said Lexi. "Are you?"

"Not scared, just a bit anxious about the red squirrel kits," said Isla. Then she whispered, barely loud enough for Lexi to hear, "And I'm worried about Tattie too."

But Lexi must've heard, because Isla felt her cold hand take hers.

A loud screeching noise in the distance made them jump.

"Do you think that's a barn owl? Remember the pellets we found," Lexi whispered.

Isla was about to reply when suddenly there was another sound: dragging footsteps outside the tent...

Lexi shot up, quivering with fear. Isla sat up beside her.

"It's M-M-Mungo!" Lexi cried. "He's coming!" She threw her arms around Isla in terror.

"Don't be daft, Lexi, Buzz made that story up!" said Isla.

But then a light shone through their tent and the zip started to lift upwards.

Lexi gasped and buried her head in her sleeping bag.

"Isla? Lexi? Are you awake?" said a familiar voice. It was Buzz! "My tent's collapsed!"

Then there was another huge gust of wind, and somewhere in the distance came a loud crack and an enormous crash.

7

Isla, Buzz and Lexi stared at each other in shock as the tents flapped and billowed.

"What was that awful noise?" Lexi cried.

"It sounded like the branch of a tree breaking off," said Buzz as Isla and Lexi struggled out of their sleeping bags and hauled on their boots.

"I think it came from the direction of the Folly," said Lexi.

"If a branch has fallen down near the Folly, we need to check that the squirrel kits are OK!" said Isla.

"Let's get Gracie," Buzz shouted to make himself heard over the wind.

They all ran over to her den and peered inside. Tucked up in her sleeping bag, Gracie lay fast asleep and snoring loudly.

"She's sleeping like a baby!" laughed Isla.

"And snoring like a wee piggy!" added Lexi. "How on earth can she manage it? It's wild out here!"

"Gracie's den is super sturdy," said Buzz. "She had the right idea!"

"Let's leave her to sleep for now," Isla decided.

There was a loud screech somewhere nearby.

"The barn owl again!" Lexi said with a yelp.

"C'mon," said Isla urgently. "We need to check on the red squirrels."

Using their torches, Isla, Lexi and Buzz wound their way carefully back to the Folly. Every so often the wind blew so hard they staggered backwards.

"Oh no!" shouted Isla. "Look!"

Shining their torches, they could see that the large branch on the Scots pine that housed the red squirrels' drey had been blown down. A mass of pine needles now covered the Folly.

"Where's the squirrels' drey?" yelled Isla.

They frantically searched the ground with their torches, but there was no sign of it.

"Let's try the other side," suggested Lexi.

They ran to the back of the Folly and once again beamed their torches.

"Nothing!" said Buzz.

Isla walked slowly back towards the front of the Folly. Even through the howling wind, she could make out faint cries.

"I can hear squeaks! Maybe the drey has fallen inside the Folly and the baby squirrels are injured!" she shouted. She quickly stepped inside and shone her torch all around, but could only see fallen branches.

"Hmm, I can't see it," said Isla.

"Oh no," said Lexi, anxiety creeping into her voice. "What are we going to do?"

Buzz, Isla and Lexi stood for a moment in the darkness, the wind shrieking in their ears and their faces lit by torchlight.

"I know what we're *not* going to do," offered Buzz.

"We're not going to panic," said Isla.

Buzz nodded. "Remember our Animal

Adventure Club Code," he said firmly. "We will deal with this problem calmly."

"And come up with a sensible plan," added Lexi, calming down.

"We need to look in and around the Folly for the squirrels and find the drey. It can't have fallen too far away," said Isla.

"What about the owl?" said Lexi.

"What do you mean?" asked Isla.

"There's a barn owl around here, remember? Squirrel kits would make a tasty meal for an owl."

"Good point," said Buzz. "Lexi, you're on owl patrol. I'm pretty sure you could scare it away if it got too close."

"Why do you think that, Buzz?" Lexi yelled, causing a bird nearby to flap out of the nearby trees. "Alright, alright," she said. "I'm the official owl scarer."

Buzz and Isla started scanning the area again with their torches, trying to work out where the drey could be. It wasn't until Isla shone her torch upwards that it dawned on her. The branch had fallen, but its top half was resting on the top of the Folly. She directed her torch beam into the branches and spotted the drey at last. Two fluffy red faces peered out at her.

But the drey was very close to the edge! *Oh no*, thought Isla. *The baby squirrels could fall out!*

"I've found the drey!" Isla said. "Now we need to make sure it's secure and check that all the kits are in there."

"But how?" said Lexi.

"I'm going to climb up the Folly," said Isla.

"Oh!" said Lexi. "I don't like the sound of this plan, Isla."

"It'll be fine," she said. "The building looks strong, and there's no sign of damage from the fallen branches. I've done tonnes of climbing before, and this really isn't very high. I'll use the window ledges for steps. Even if I do fall, it'll be onto soft moss."

"You're right, Isla, it's not that high," agreed Buzz. "I'll shine the torch up so you can see where you're going."

Lexi looked doubtful, but Isla was calm

and very determined. *I have to rescue those squirrel kits,* she thought.

Isla slipped her foot onto the lower window ledge, and then hoisted herself up to the next one, further along. It was pitch-black and there was no moon, so Buzz shone his torch to light each step of the way.

She moved carefully along the higher ledge. From here, she could just reach the drey. The fork of the branch was right beside her now and the football-sized drey was hanging on it. Isla peered in and made out two fluffy little faces staring back at her.

"There are only two!" she shouted down. Isla gently put her hand on the drey. "Don't worry, wee guys," she said softly. "I'll make sure you're safe."

But all of a sudden, there was a huge gust of wind and the drey came away in Isla's hands!

"Um, guys," shouted Isla, "the drey's come loose! There's nowhere safe to put it down up here, and I can't get down with it in my hands. I'm stuck!"

"Oh, I don't like this," said Lexi anxiously. "I don't like this one bit."

"I'm sure it'll be fine," said Buzz. "Just hold on, Isla!"

Isla could feel her legs getting a little wobbly. What if she fell, still holding the drey?

8

Isla was stuck near the top of the Folly, with the red squirrel kits' drey in her hands. How would she get down?

Suddenly a welcome voice shouted from below.

"Right, what have I missed?" It was Gracie, wearing her head torch! She marched towards them and then looked up. "What are you doing up there, Isla?"

Isla breathed a sigh of relief.

"Just in time, Gracie!" said Lexi. "We have a wee problem."

"Er, could you come and help?" asked Isla. "The drey came loose in my hands

and now I'm stuck."

"Buzz, go on my shoulders," said Gracie, bending down.

"Great plan!" said Buzz, swinging a leg over Gracie's head. Lexi took his torch and helped to steady him as Gracie lifted him up. Buzz reached up, took the drey out of Isla's shaking hands and handed it to Lexi as Gracie lowered him down.

Next, Gracie guided Isla's feet back down the wall of the Folly to the safety of the ground.

"Phew!" said Isla. "Thanks, Gracie, you always know what to do in a crisis."

"Sorry I was late!" she said.

"Better late than never," said Buzz.

They placed the drey inside one of the Folly's window spaces, where fallen branches would protect it. It was up off the ground and tucked well away from predators.

"Chilli and Spice look cosy in there," said Buzz, peering inside.

"But that means Scarlet is missing!" said Gracie.

"Now the drey is lower down, she might be able to find her way back in," suggested Lexi.

"But where is she?" Isla wondered. "Let's look in the Folly again."

They all crept carefully inside the Folly, which was littered with fallen Scots pine branches.

Buzz slowly flashed his torch around. "I don't think she's here," he said.

Then there was a small squeak.

"Wait," said Isla. "Look in there!"

The tiny squirrel kit was stuck deep inside a pile of tangled branches and pine needles.

"Poor wee thing! She sounds like she's in distress," said Gracie. "And she's trapped."

"She could be injured from the fall too," said Buzz. "I think we need to get Lisa to help us with this."

"Let's get that walkie-talkie," said Gracie.

"Yes," said Isla, "that's a good plan."

The Animal Adventure Club headed back round the island to their tents, but they couldn't find the walkie-talkie.

"I remember Lisa giving you the walkie-talkie, Gracie. Where is it now?" said Buzz.

Everyone turned to look at her.

"I can't remember," said Gracie, chewing a fingernail. "I think I put it next to our food supplies, before they were loaded onto the boat."

"Maybe it fell under the seat in the boat!" suggested Isla.

They ran down to where the boat was tied up and shone their torches over the lochside, but the boat wasn't there.

"I'm sure I tied the boat up here," said Gracie.

"Yes, I thought you did too," said Isla.

"Well, it's not here now..." said Buzz.

"Look!" said Lexi, shining her torch on a tree. A piece of rope trailed from it, but the boat was nowhere to be seen.

The Animal Adventure Club were stranded on Mungo's Island.

9

Isla, Buzz, Gracie and Lexi looked out at the dark loch, trying their best to spot the missing boat. If the walkie-talkie was still inside, they had no way of letting Lisa know that one of the squirrel kits needed help.

"Did you tie the boat up properly, Gracie?" asked Buzz. "Remember, you tied a different knot to the one Lisa said..."

Even in the darkness, Isla could see the flash of anger in Gracie's eyes.

"Of course I did!" she snapped at Buzz. She folded her arms tightly. "Why are you all staring at me?"

There was a moment of complete silence.

Then Gracie wailed, "This is a *total* disaster." She put her head in her hands. "You're right. It's all my fault! Maybe I did get the knot wrong, like I've messed everything else up today. I'm so sorry I've let you all down."

"Wait, what? It's not your fault!" said Isla defiantly. "What gave you that idea?"

"Yes, it is," Gracie insisted. "I tied up the boat with a different knot from the one Lisa suggested. I didn't get the tents put up before the rain came, I didn't *insist* that we put our tents in a more sheltered place so they wouldn't get blown over, I forgot the tent pegs. I slept through the squirrel rescue! And now I've left the walkie-talkie on a boat that's floated away! It's *all* my fault, and I'm the one who keeps going on about being a survival expert! I'm useless!"

"Wait a minute," said Lexi. "It was the rest of us who wanted to explore before putting up the tents, and it was Buzz and me who wanted to pitch the tents near the loch. And the weather changes all the time in Scotland. It isn't anybody's fault, Gracie!"

"Hang on," said Isla, shining her torch on the tree. "You tied a great knot! Look, it's still really secure – it was the rope that broke! It must've been old and frayed. And we both should've checked the tent pegs, Gracie. I was distracted when we were packing because I was worrying about Tattie, so it's my fault too."

"You were sensible and built a brilliant den, and none of us helped you," said Lexi.

"And you saved the day with the squirrel rescue!" added Isla.

Big tears were rolling down Gracie's face, and Isla put her arm around her friend's shoulder.

Buzz said quietly, "Actually, if anyone should be saying sorry, it's me. I've just remembered that Lisa handed me the walkie-talkie when I was on the boat. I put it down at my feet and it slipped under the seat."

"It's alright, Buzz," said Gracie. "We were all so excited when we got here that *none* of us checked we'd brought it onto the island." She wiped the tears from her face. "Thanks for making me feel better, guys.

I thought you were all really cross with me."

"Hey," said Lexi, grabbing Gracie by the shoulders. "We're the Animal Adventure Club, remember? We're a team!"

The wind had died down and the clouds parted. A bright moon lit up their faces as they stood together on the shore of Loch Dooey. Then, letting go of Gracie, Lexi put her fist into the middle of the group and they all joined her in a fist bump.

"We can do this!" said Isla.

"I don't know how, but we'll think of something!" said Gracie.

"OK, let's look at the facts," said Buzz. "We're stranded, but we're safe."

"One of the squirrel kits is trapped and possibly injured," said Isla.

"We need to get in touch with Lisa. But how?" asked Lexi, sitting down on a rock and drumming her fingers on it.

Buzz's face lit up. "Hey, Lexi, that tapping reminds me of Morse code. Dot dot, dash dash! Remember, Gracie?"

"Oh yeah!" But then she bit her lip anxiously. "But what if it doesn't work?"

"It will," Buzz replied firmly.

Isla squeezed Gracie's hand. "Gracie, you've got this."

Gracie nodded. Buzz handed her his

torch, and she ran over to the water's edge directly opposite where Lisa was camping on the far shore.

"Lexi, give us a couple of your ear-splittingly loud whistles," Gracie asked. "They might just carry on the wind and help waken Lisa."

Lexi slipped her forefinger and thumb into her mouth and blew. They all quickly put their fingers in their ears.

Then Gracie reached into her backpack and pulled out a notebook, pencil and her Morse code book. She clicked her torch on and off in a pattern: three short flashes, followed by three long ones and then three short ones again.

"What are you saying in Morse code, Gracie?" asked Buzz.

"SOS," she replied. "Save Our Souls: it's

the signal that means you need help. It goes: Dot dot dot, dash dash dash, dot dot dot. The dots are really short flashes, the dashes are a wee bit longer." Gracie clicked her torch on and off, making the pattern with the beam of light.

dot   dot   dot   dash   dash   dash   dot   dot   dot

Then they waited.

Nothing: just darkness and the vague outline of trees in the distance, swaying in the wind. There was a call from a bird as it darted overhead.

"Come on, Lisa." said Isla quietly, chewing her fingernails.

"Try again, Gracie," said Buzz. "The wind

has died down a bit, so Lisa might hear Lexi's whistles."

Lexi whistled again and Gracie repeated her torch message.

They all watched the other side of the loch, waiting...

"Look!" cried Lexi. "Lisa's sending a message back!"

A series of lights flashed back. Gracie scribbled the sequence into her notebook, then decoded the message.

"*On... my... way!*" said Gracie. "She's coming!"

"The survival expert saves the day!" said Buzz triumphantly. "I'm sorry for ever doubting Morse code, Gracie. It's totally brilliant!"

10

The Animal Adventure Club cheered as Lisa's boat rowed towards them. The wind had dropped now and the moon glittered in the ripples across Loch Dooey.

"Are we glad to see you!" said Gracie as Lisa climbed out of the boat to join them.

They quickly explained everything to her.

"My goodness," Lisa said. "What a night you've had! Well done for your quick thinking on using Morse code, Gracie. Now, let's go and find this squirrel kit."

Once they had trekked round to the

Folly, Lisa quickly assessed the problem.

"Isla, it was a good idea to keep the drey somewhere safe, sheltered and off the ground. But you're right, there's an injured kit stuck in the fallen branches. It's pretty hard to get in and see, but I can hear it's not happy. Buzz, pass me my rucksack, and Gracie, go and grab a jumper from your rucksack. Do you have some kind of box I could use?"

"Um, a biscuit tin?" suggested Buzz. "It's completely empty now..."

Gracie chuckled and ran off to grab the jumper and the tin.

Lisa pulled out a pair of thick gloves and some small wire clippers from her rucksack. She slipped on the gloves, explaining, "I don't want a nasty bite from a baby squirrel."

"Scarlet," said Lexi. "We've named them all."

"Well, let's see if we can rescue little Scarlet," said Lisa. She manoeuvred herself into the Folly through the arched door and began clipping smaller branches so she could reach further in. All the while, the Animal Adventure Club could hear terrified squeaks from the baby squirrel.

"Nearly there, little one," said Lisa. "Do you have that jumper, Gracie?"

"Here," said Gracie, spreading it out on the ground.

Lisa began slowly backing out of the Folly, clutching the tiny red squirrel in her gloves. She placed her on the jumper and scooped her up.

"Here's the tin," said Buzz, pulling the lid off.

Soon Scarlet was cosy and safe in her new biscuit-tin bed.

"Buzz, could you have a quick look at her? Here, take my gloves," said Lisa. "She doesn't seem too anxious."

Buzz popped on the gloves and looked carefully at Scarlet. "I think she's broken her leg, it's not lying straight," he said. "The poor wee thing must be in pain."

"Yes, I thought that too," said Lisa. "Let's get her back over to the lodge, keep her comfortable and we'll contact Strathdooey Wildlife Hospital in the morning. They'll help her get well again."

The Animal Adventure Club all nodded.

"I don't think we can leave the other squirrel kits here to fend for themselves," said Lisa. "Normally, I'd say wait and watch from a distance to see if the mother returns, but I think it's unlikely she will. Anyway, the drey has moved, so she might not find them."

"Could we bring the whole drey?" suggested Isla. "It's strong enough. And then we won't have to handle the kits."

"Great idea," said Lisa. She and Isla carefully lifted the drey from the window of the Folly. Chilli and Spice were fast asleep inside.

"Grab your sleeping bags and bring them too," added Lisa, carrying the drey. "You can stay in the lodge and come back for the rest of your stuff in the morning."

As Lisa rowed them back across the moonlit Loch Dooey, Scarlet snuggled down inside the tin and seemed quite happy to be carried by Buzz, while Isla and Gracie kept an eye on Chilli and Spice.

"Don't worry, wee thing," said Isla leaning over to Scarlet. "You'll all be safe very soon."

Lexi yawned and stared over at the cute bundle in the biscuit tin. "We should've called her Gingernut!"

Back at the lodge, the Animal Adventure Club and Lisa set up camp, laying their sleeping bags on the floor. Lexi and Gracie made everyone a steaming mug of hot chocolate, while Lisa, Isla and Buzz placed the drey into the large crate the rangers used for injured animals. Then they settled Scarlet into a smaller cage beside them. They popped a hot-water bottle wrapped in a blanket beside her, and soon she curled up her tail and bundled herself into a ball. She looked drowsy, but every so often she gave a little squeak.

"Poor wee thing," said Isla.

"She'll be OK," said Buzz. "At least she's warm and comfortable and will soon get the care she needs."

"It's not long until morning," said Lisa, looking at her watch. "I've already texted

Tomasz, my vet friend at Strathdooey Wildlife Hospital. I'm sure he'll be over first thing."

Suddenly there was a ping on Isla's phone.

"I've had a text message and a photo from my mum!" she said, turning her phone around to show everyone.

"She must've sent it last night, but there was no reception on the island. Tattie's perked up and is back playing on his wheel. The medicine must've worked!"

"That's brilliant, Isla," said Gracie with a smile. "He looks loads better."

"You all look exhausted," said Lisa. "C'mon, off to bed."

Soon, everyone was fast asleep. Even Scarlet.

11

The next morning, the sun was shining. Tomasz the vet from the wildlife hospital arrived very early. Buzz was thrilled to help him put a tiny cast on Scarlet's leg. Then they popped her into the same cage as her sisters. They looked very happy to be reunited.

"Well done, Buzz," said Tomasz. "We'll keep an eye on Scarlet, but she'll be fine. The others look really healthy too, so I'll just show you how to top up their food with milk. Hopefully in a few weeks we can release them back into the reserve."

After Tomasz had left, everyone sat

down to enjoy some juice and toast.

"So, you were right about Scarlet," said Lisa to Buzz. "She did have a broken leg."

"Aw," said Lexi, "poor wee thing."

"But well done, Buzz," said Gracie. "You were spot on!"

Buzz went a little pink and smiled. "Thanks, Gracie."

With the squirrels now safe, the Animal Adventure Club headed back to Mungo's Island to pack away their tents and tidy up. They found their boat, which had drifted over to the Roman Fort side of the loch and was caught up in some reeds there. They also found the walkie-talkie tucked under one of the seats.

"The midges are back." Buzz slapped furiously once again. "Why do they always go for me?"

"That's the tent all folded tight," said Isla. "I just need to squeeze it back into its bag. Pass it over will you, Gracie."

Gracie lifted up the bag. "Oh!" she said. "Look! It's ripped down the side."

"That's why the wee bag of tent pegs fell out!" said Isla. "See, I knew it wasn't your fault."

Gracie grinned.

"Let's go and check on the water voles before we leave," said Buzz.

As they walked around the island, they stopped to look at the old Scots pine.

"Even though it lost some big branches, at least it's still standing," said Buzz.

"Hey, what's that bird sitting on the top?" said Lexi looking up. "Er, it's very big and I'm pretty sure it's not an owl."

Buzz lifted his binoculars to his eyes to take a good look at the large bird sitting proudly on what was left of the old Scots pine.

"Oh my goodness," he said. "It's a hawk!"

Buzz passed the binoculars around so they could all take a good look.

"I think it's a goshawk," added Isla.

It stared fiercely down at the Animal

Adventure Club. It had a grey-brown and white striped chest, white eyebrows, and yellow legs with sharp talons.

"Oh wow!" said Gracie. "It's beautiful."

"Maybe the goshawk has a nest in the tree too," said Buzz.

"That might explain what spooked the squirrel kits' mum," said Isla. "Goshawks are a predator of red squirrels. I think we saved Chilli, Spice and Scarlet from becoming dinner."

"Yup, but now the goshawk's hungry," said Gracie. "Maybe it's got babies to feed."

"Sorry Mr or Mrs Goshawk," said Lexi. "It's a tough world!"

And as if hearing this, the goshawk spread its huge wings and soared into the sky.

"Wow," said Buzz.

"Now what about our water vole friends," said Isla, walking towards the shore where they left the crates.

"I guess they were safely in their burrows when it was windy last night," said Gracie. "Ooh and look!" She pointed to some soft mud and a pile of nibbled reeds. "I think we've found their dining room!"

"Star-shaped prints, just like you said," said Lexi, bending down for a closer look.

"And the bite marks on the grassy stalks look about 45 degrees," said Isla. "You can actually see the wee teeth marks. Well, it looks as though they've made themselves right at home!"

"We can add it to our poster," said Buzz. "Animals you might spot at Pittendooey Nature Reserve: water voles!"

Then Isla signalled to the others. A water vole was pottering through the vegetation nearby. It stopped and began munching on a piece of long grass, gripping it with its tiny paws.

"Aw," whispered Lexi. "He's having his breakfast."

"That reminds me," said Buzz quietly. "I'm starving!"

Back at the lodge, Chilli and Spice were chasing each other around their cage while Scarlet rested. The Animal Adventure Club watched them, grinning.

"Well, they're certainly happy," said Lisa, glancing out the window. "Oh, that looks like your mum's car, Isla."

"Yay!" squealed Isla, picking up her rucksack and tent.

As they all headed out to the car, Isla's mum was standing with the boot open, waiting to load their stuff into the back. She looked inside and gasped.

"Oh no!" she said, holding up a small bag. "The tent pegs!"

"Don't worry, Mum," said Isla, showing her mum the tear on the tent bag. "Gracie just built a den, like she said she would. It was no problem!"

"No, it wasn't a problem," said Buzz with a straight face. "And neither was all our stuff getting soaked in the rain."

"Or the wind blowing a massive branch

off a tree," said Gracie with a shrug.

"Or a baby red squirrel falling from its nest and breaking its leg," added Lexi, folding her arms.

"Or the boat drifting away," said Isla, "with the walkie-talkie inside."

"Leaving us stranded," added Buzz.

"Nope. No problems for us," said Isla with a twinkle in her eye.

Isla's mum's eyebrows got higher and higher.

Then unable to keep their faces straight any longer, everyone burst out laughing.

"I'll tell you what was a problem though," said Buzz, scratching his head furiously.

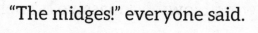

"The midges!" everyone said.

"Right, Animal Adventure Club, it sounds like you've got a lot to tell me!" said Isla's mum, shaking her head. "And then, Isla MacLeod, there's a small mouse waiting for you at home."

"Aw, Tattie!" said Isla. "I can't wait to see him. This has been the best weekend ever!"

The End

Come exploring with the

ANIMAL ADVENTURE CLUB CODE

MEMBERS:

Isla MacLeod

Buzz (Robert) Campbell

Gracie Munroe

Lexi Budge

OUR MISSION IS TO TAKE CARE OF ALL LIVING CREATURES.

CODE

1. We will treat all animals from bugs to badgers with respect. **Even midges and spiders!**

2. We will look after the natural world and respect the countryside.

3. We will never drop litter.

And we'll recycle any we find lying around

4. We will have fun outdoors!

5. We will always work as a team.

6. We will approach problems calmly and make a sensible plan.

7. We will ask adults for advice when we need to.

8. We will always be prepared and pack a torch, map, compass and waterproof jacket before going on patrol.

9. We will always welcome new members.

10. We will always have hot chocolate and a packet of biscuits in the lodge.

Preferably custard creams!

SIGNED: Buzz   Isla

Gracie   Lexi

How to build a den

Building a den from fallen branches, twigs and leaves is great fun! Find a clearing in a forest and have a go.

You will need...

- Two long, sturdy sticks with a Y shape at one end
- One very long stick (about the same height as you) with a Y shape at one end
- Lots of smaller sticks, as needed
- Moss and leaves to stuff gaps, as needed

1. Make the entrance to your den by taking the two long sticks with the Y-shapes at the ends and slotting them together to make an A shape.

2. Next, prop the Y-shaped end of the long stick – or ridge pole – into the ground and rest the other end on the top of the entrance to your den.

It needs to be sturdy!

3. To make the walls, gather up lots of small branches.
Place them close together along the length of the ridge pole.

4. Finally, weave in leaves or thinner, bendier branches.
Add some moss too, to make your den super cosy!

How to use Morse code

Morse code is a way of sending messages using dots and dashes that represent letters of the alphabet. It is named after Samuel Morse, an American inventor who helped develop it back in the 1830s.

Morse code can be sent as a series of sounds or even as flashes of light. By switching your torch on and off, you could send messages in the dark to a friend. *Just like I did with Lisa!*

A dot is a short flash (about a second long).
A dash is a longer flash (around three seconds long).

Can you decode these messages?

This is the Morse code alphabet. Grab a notebook and a pencil, and decode these Animal Adventure Club words

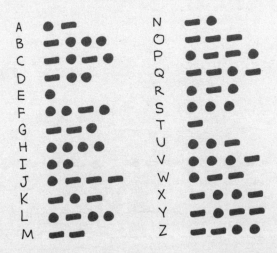

1.

•—• • —••

<u>R</u> ___ ___

••• ————•— ••—• ••

___ ___ ___ ___

•—• •—•— • •—••

___ ___ ___ ___

2.

•—•• ——— —•—• ••••

<u>L</u> ___ ___ ___

—•• ——— ——— • —•—•

___ ___ ___ ___ ___

3.

•—— •— — • •—•

<u>W</u> ___ ___ ___ ___

••• —— —— •—•• •

___ ___ ___ ___

Red Squirrels

Babies = Kittens

What do we look like?
- We have reddish fur and tails, and tufty ears.
- When we are born, we don't have any hair at all!

Where do we live?
- We live in nests called dreys.
- Dreys are balls made of twigs. Inside, leaves, moss and grass keep us warm.
- Three-quarters of British red squirrels live in Scotland.

What do we like to eat?
- We love to eat pine seeds. In one year, one of us can eat the seeds of 20,000 cones!

- We also love nuts, fungi, shoots and berries.
- Occasionally we eat birds' eggs.
- We can tell if a nut is rotten inside its shell just
  by shaking it in our paws!

Fun facts

- We are rare: there are only about 140,000 of us in Britain.
  (There are more than 2 million grey squirrels!)
- When we are babies, we need our mums to feed us
  until we are 10 weeks old.
- We like an afternoon nap, especially when the
  weather is warm.
- We can swim, but it's hard work!

Red Squirrel footprints

Water Voles

Babies = Pups

What do we look like?

- We have round faces, small ears and chestnut-brown coats.
- In Scotland, some of us have black fur.
- We have furry feet and tails, and small black eyes.
- We are sometimes confused with the brown rat.

Where do we live?

- We live near water: rivers, streams, canals, lochs, ponds and marshes.
- We like to be near lots of lush, overgrown vegetation.
- We dig burrows with lots of interconnecting tunnels into grassy banks.

What do we like to eat?

- We mainly eat grass, reeds and water plants.
- Sometimes we eat buds, bulbs and bark.
- Very occasionally we might eat insects.

Fun facts

- We are strong swimmers and can float on the surface of water.
- Although we are semi-aquatic, we don't have webbed feet!
- We poo in little piles called 'latrines'.
- We bite stems of grass at a 45-degree angle.
- A famous water vole is Ratty from *The Wind in the Willows* by Kenneth Grahame.

Water Vole footprints

Goshawks

What do we look like?

- We are large birds of prey.
- We have red eyes, white eyebrows and a fierce expression.
- We have pale-grey and white stripy bodies.
- We have long yellow legs and sharp talons.

Where do we live?

- We live in woodlands and forests.
- We build our nests close to tree trunks.
- Our nests are reused for several years.

What do we like to eat?

• We eat smaller birds like wood pigeons and crows.
• We also eat small mammals, such as rabbits and squirrels.

Fun facts

• We perform a 'sky-dance' with lots of dramatic
  swoops when we're trying to attract a mate!
• We like to hunt in woodland and can fly at up to
  40 kilometres an hour.
• We can easily weave through lots of trees and are
  sometimes called the 'phantoms of the forest'.

Goshawk footprints

Read on to discover another
brilliant animal adventure!

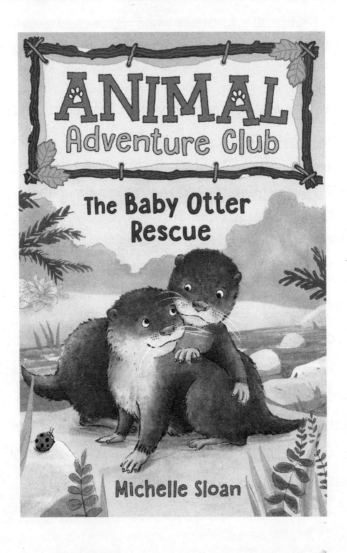

The otter cub's tufty dark-brown fur was wet and its tiny webbed toes poked out from under its tummy. Its long tail snaked along the soaking-wet ground. When it looked up and saw Isla, it let out another cry. It was very upset and frightened.

"Oh, you poor thing," whispered Isla. "You're just a tiny wee cub. Far too young to be without your mum."

Isla backed away from the window very slowly, over to Gracie's bed.

"Gracie, this time you have to wake up!" she said urgently.

Gracie stirred. "Too sleepy," she mumbled.

"I need your help! There's a baby otter at your back door."

Gracie shot up. "What?" she said. "An otter?" She scrambled out of bed and the two girls headed downstairs. They could hear the crying from the kitchen. Even Haggis the guinea pig looked alarmed, peering out of his crate anxiously.

As Gracie unlocked and opened the back door very carefully and slowly, the whining got a little louder. When the door was fully open, they saw the mewling cub looking up at them. "We need to keep very still and calm," whispered Isla. "So that the little cub knows it can trust us." The girls kept their breathing steady and soon the cub stopped squeaking. Then it flopped down on the step, keeping its eyes on them. The girls knelt down to observe the otter from a safe distance. It had a black button nose and whiskers that curved around its mouth.

"Oh my goodness," whispered Gracie. "I've never seen anything so cute. Lexi would love this!"

"It's adorable," Isla agreed, "and even cuter close up! But remember it's a wild animal. It's got very sharp little teeth and claws."

"True," said Gracie. "But where's its mum? I don't know much about otters, but this one doesn't look old enough to be out on its own."

The otter cub cocked its head to one side, as if it were listening intently to what they were saying. Then it let out another long, mournful wail.

"I wonder why it's come to your door?" asked Isla. "Maybe it's hungry and it smelled the fish fingers we had for tea last night!"

"Maybe," chuckled Gracie. "But I don't think we can give it fish fingers! What on earth should we feed you, wee chum?"

"You're right, I think it might be too young for fish. It's probably still having its mother's milk," said Isla.

"Its mum might be around somewhere," said Gracie, looking across her back garden. "Perhaps we should wait for the mum to come back for her baby."

"But if we leave it too long, the cub might get really, *really* hungry," said Isla.

"Or maybe it's not hungry after all. Maybe it's crying because it's injured," added Gracie. "Let's ask my mum and dad, they'll know what to do."

The story continues in
The Baby Otter Rescue

What if I find an injured wild animal?

The Animal Adventure Club have lots of exciting encounters with wild animals, but remember that in real life you should always ask a grown-up for help. If you find an injured wild animal, call a local vet or wildlife organisation for advice.

Top Tips

Be sensible and cautious. Stay back and watch the animal for a while to see how badly injured it is. Wild animals can scratch and bite.

Tell a grown-up, or call a vet or wildlife organisation for help.

If you are helping a grown-up collect a wild animal, you can suggest that they line a well-ventilated cardboard box with newspaper or towels. Next, put on gloves, lift the animal (keeping it away from your face), and quickly put it into the box.

There are some injured animals you should never try to handle: deer, seals, wild boar, otters, badgers, foxes, snakes, birds of prey (including owls), swans, geese, herons or gulls. Instead, call a vet or wildlife organisation.